Mister Animal Bible

PHILLO

A thankful message to all readers I thank you for taking interest in my Book.

Thanks once again feel free to be artist and contribute to the future of publishing Art for a Animal Charity. With contributing freely.

Phillo.

Mister Animal Bible

Once in Apouce in the smalls of a city they're sat a cast of shadow With shuddered looks a man wearing winter casual. His breath giving to smoke he shook his Head chilled by the airs surrounding his Eyeful view He sat Back scowling with freezing Ice winds.

He smoked trying to warm his hands swearing at life for never finishing the final touches of Difference. Ideas Wondrous too many in thought throwing his cigar away he sat and looked at a Distant Cloud hovering In the Far distance he sighed.

Sat by himself waiting for nothings he browsed on the idea of going to Another County poor as poor his empty pocket he looked in the trees thoughtfully Thinking about his Terrible disorganized life. "What the hell am I doing sitting Here with sod all to do but consider the best place to go".

The entire world and their sat with his smiling teeth he looked at the snow Distanced by his grin he awaited just wanting to go home he was just standing when the Cloud shot above him there was a thunderclap a bang like he never heard in his life. He Fell on his butt shocked.

The snow fell past his eyes, breathing heavenly; he wiped his face and a bright Light with a Dark shadow rounded of figure appeared in front of him standing he was wearing a Robe and smiled. Jacob sat and store the figure moved slightly Jacob froze asking who he Was he replied 'Noah'.

Jacob tried to quickly escape Noah reassured him calmly with words and Gestured. Sitting he looked at Jacob and asked him to work for him and the animal kingdom. Jacob Shook his head saying 'since I don't know you their isn't anything I Can do'.

'And. meeting like this Isn't the best way'.

"What the hell are you doing I didn't ask for a spook for Christmas can't you just Let me go I Don't want to see you".

"Listen Jacob I have a Job for you, theirs a virgin I Know and she's pregnant and between me and the gods; she's very important now don't ask Me how, but she pregnant and Wondering town. And she needs a man. Now you're the man And I'm going to propose a gift".

"And what is this gift I can even remember going out with a virgin and since. I've got No money Ill Ask what's the business?

You write books and I want a book called the 'Animal Bible' you write it as A Story and ill give you all the money you want. "Are you Sure, I need money now and I want some Comfort called a decent life". "Jacob you will be Given gifts and you can have all the 'cigars' 'wine' And 'Meat' you ever dreamt of"? "But I'm a vegetarian".

"Jacob ill think of something otherwise? Just Understand That She is pregnant And she passing you in three minutes so ill see you again just invite her for coffee and the Universe will do the rest".

The clouds disappeared leaving quickly the Sun came out the snow remained and Jacob Looked round the park people passed smiling chatting; a dog running around chasing A football.

Jacob Sat he laughed sniggering at first slightly cautious then roared in laughter. Calming his voice he was Giggling, Staring at nothings with a glazed eye he went quiet. Sat Holding his forehead in disbelief he started crying. Whimpering he held his breath, looked At the sun a smile.

Jacob then stood he looked around and sat down again, a young lady of about Twenty years of Age walk to the bench and stopped she said she was lost she was pregnant And she was cold, Jacob told her where she was and sat down she asked his name he Offered his coat and sat again he told her where He lived and she smiled saying she had Nowhere to stay He asked her to call in for coffee, she agreed. Jacob smiled and they Walked slowly towards the nearest street which wasn't far Away.

He introduced himself and spoke of the area and how people were so considerate She Hesitated as he wouldn't stop speak he seemed fascinated and she kept her words quite And given time she knew he was a kindly man from a country that lived with memories of Fatherhood if it wasn't England it was Greece and he did after all have slightly tanned Features she admired the way he walked and they arrived at the door of a large house with Master windows, the door opened with a key and they entered a staircase with carpets And walked the stairs.

"Come in", Virtue walked in and Jacob stood as she entered "very Nice, cosy and You have so Many things all those books and that's a computer?" "Yes I've had it for five Months I bought it from a Friend he knows how to look after them and lives nearby". "Do You work with computers" "No I write Books I've struggled for years I've started again, Would you like a coffee?"

Coffee was made and he asked if she would like some music on, What music was a question He considered, anything you like I've boxes of music they Eventually spoke about differences and meanwhile put soft instrumental music to calm of Atmosphere."

Where are you from" Jacob asked assuming that she was homeless and in Need Of a place to sleep.

She Replied "A house that I lived in for the years I worked for Sisters of clergy then after I left I lived with a man I deeply loved and he found a job that Left me a choice to stay in England or to move with him to The American city of New York. I couldn't bear the idea so he sold the house and he went meanwhile I've Wondered the Streets. Since last week. I've no friends here slept in a hostel meanwhile".

Chapter 1

So NOW YOU KNOW ME and I will give you a introductory of myself", I've been in this city for Ten years moving around due to bad neighbours and I've lived here for two years writing For Fifteen years and have never published until now I have settled I have found friends and people That can really help, now I'm going to start all over again. "What happened to your old books"? "I Threw them away in Despair I just couldn't imagine editing them and keeping them wasn't intended I Became ill as I was under a lot of pressure", "You threw them away! What a shame, maybe it was a Good thing; it's always good to start Afresh". "Your right, I Always knew what I wanted but it took Years to realize what I was writing and I Was driven by money That I didn't have and I was confused so now I stick with the Thought of 'One Book' everything is the Book I'm writing and nothing diverts My Mind. "So you have found the secret of writing and you're becoming well known for words Written in English, so sparing the nonsense of those years"?

Yes I'm improving; have you written A book of your own, maybe you could help I'm in the middle of a play and friends are helping Eventually ill get there its just deciding my destiny and I think theirs always room for another 'Inspirit' Writer".

"I've never completed a book however I have saved my stories their in my mothers bedroom, When a friend moved in she emptied the bedroom and they were left there". "I've seen one of my Stories on TV, commentary it wasn't brilliant but it had a place of experience. I didn't patent them I Aught to and will one day now I know you, you could help me".

"I will help in fact, do you want a drink of something, I'm going to have a beer, and you can Have Coffee Tea or a relaxing drink of chocolate perhaps. "I will thanks", "Chocolate then it is and Look At the music I'll put it on for you." "Ill be back in a minute, the bathrooms through there, clean You up I think theirs a bottle of perfume in their I bought it especially for my female friends Use the White towels there for you".

"I'll sit and wait till you do all the work I'm hungry though I could do with some food do you Have a snack"? Hollering from the kitchen he came through the kitchen door "I've got sandwiches 'Tuna' 'Prawns' or just salad?" "Just salad with mayonnaise and pepper can I come through"?

"You might take your time explaining some time when you have 'Time and space' because it sandwich Just isn't squeezing in my brain appetite'. Anyway dead salad is better that salad running on legs. Have you Decided what you want" "I've got plenty, I just can't find my mayonnaise it looks like salad cream Mayonnaise just isn't the dresser.

"Let's go through and sit ill put the music on you can tell me more about you". "I think Ill have a time of my life here theirs so much to see in your apartment I've never seen half of the Ornaments I'm always preoccupied. You will have to show me around. I've collected all my ornaments In charity Shops round the city and I can see a bargain from distanced windows I almost sense it and it Might be slightly compulsive a habit but a controlled one with place for anything wondrous as the World with No place to go".

"You must complement yourself assuming the collection of gift's as I would describe I can See an eye of beauty in your beholding the statues you have will always give you friends of Considering giving Gifts to".

"If I could I would harbour more articles and advertise them as a sale otherwise I would hold A sale and proudly advertise well before I think I could be surprised at the gathering I receive".

However let's talk about you you're saying you have nowhere to stay, what is your plan". Jacob held Lips remembering the vision of Noah seeing a glimmer of a smile with a cigar held a ten-foot stature Eyes holding his memory as if to assume his words carried.

Virtue gazed for moment breathing Aspiration Give time she asking herself looked at the floor And said she had nowhere to go she then changed the Subject and referred to an Icon on the table near To Jacob she pointed saying "G.O.D". Jacob smiled "Yes" a book I haven't quite finished. "Gods a favourite pastime of Eternal Heaven A 'heart beat' with a name in the Book of Suns. She Smiled and carried on eating.

Jacob however was preoccupied by his inner eye he was observing the computer in his other room tickled by his premonition he thought writing the book's Animal Bible would be a continuation For other's thinking of a letter referred to others round the world he would pleasingly keepsake. He would soon sent as a complete book. A miracle in a mirror of his very own disbelief.

Chapter 2

"I THINK I OWE YOU AN apology for being inconvenient, I know I would have done the same for You and being female you're quite a person in fact I know more about you that you think". "And how Is This? "My family have a company and I've seen your book's even though you haven't published Them, I was there when they were published and I have an Uncle that works for city 'Observe' as the Company is called and I have noticed you the day I saw you I thought I would like to see you".

"So your saying' my dustbin has published my works, you mean to tell me that you edited my 'Terrible Masterpieces' the day I see the books ill wait. Are you sure you want to carry on? "We will Talk about it later you look like you need another beer the cigarettes seem to be another option". "Your name seems to be a little to close for comfort and since you know me I think ill ask for you to Stay, you probably did a profile check and a body scan isn't the world nicely hidden in eyes for Humans Only".

"I do say that complements were regarded and my family considered paying you and now I Know you we can safely consider you will be paid it may sound like a conspiracy and yet it is, the World is changing and the though of offering freedom is very near to expectation, in fact there are Representatives in line of preparation".

"So it couldn't be that I'm going to be paid and I might Assume you're going to surprise me and do you know I might even ask who you really are and is that By Any chance my baby in the eyes of your superficial intelligence and most had hidden friends".

And your family company they seem to have everything what else do they do and how long Have they been up and running it sounds like a very interesting place it isn't under the city is it?" "It's Been established for longer than you think its now in its best moments, however I've never been Involved I left it to other members of the family but I do know that one day I will ask about your Money my father would be glad to give it to you a well-paid man with a surprise that he never Expected".

"It certainly will be a day ill keep it in mind I might even consider your staying here as a true Dream of friend in vanity considering my own image in godly heavens known as Forth Every Gifts Given to the friends I never knew". "I say it's called love at first sight".

"You know I almost agreed With that and how are you going to explain the baby, don't tell me it was a angelical deed fallen from Self-loved indulging". "That's almost funny you aught to be a comedian you could make laughter seem Like a pastime". "I won't ask about the baby 'what are you doing tonight theirs good film's on tonight Non-violent or we could watch a DVD? "Let me show you round the Apartment".

"Here's the bathroom it small but convenience and it's very warm the heating in here is Slumber it's a vaporizer it puts steam in the air enjoyable, nicely decorated and clean".

"Come Through to the bedroom where you will be sleeping it's the spare room it's pleasant And smells slightly of unused airs and theirs a music system and TV. And a small table for your use".

"Yes I like it was it designed for a female? It has female qualities I like the bedding. Very pleasant". "Sit on it sense the air's of dream's it's the best mattress I saw far more comfortable than mine had to Be double and it's in the right colours for the room suited with all the trimming's".

"Standing Virtue Smiled and looked at the furnishing admiring the differences in the room's Considering "A very nice Choice of room's you must tell me where you got them from one day, do you Consider yourself to be a traveller"? "Yes travelling is good and yet I never really thought it was good At the Time but now I've better things to do and since I've lived here I've stayed very much put".

"Let's go through to the sitting room and talk about tonight I prepare a perfect meal for two I'll go to the supermarket if you want anything I'll go for you". "I'll adjust to the surroundings I love The Bay window with the cushion's I'll wait for you". "Help your self to food and drink ill be ten Minutes".

Jacob then commenced to the local shop uttering to himself aimlessly smiling assuming the Cold airs he entered the shop he glanced over his shoulder, as he looked he saw a man in a robe white Light shone round him he looked away and realized what he was seeing he looked back the robe Walked Round a corner muttering to himself he asked if the shopkeeper saw him, he shrugged his Shoulders and asked for money, Jacob was shaking slightly too much drink he assumed he walked Back home everyone was being unusually happy smiling regarding the sun came out as he entered the House he lived in.

"Hello I'm back are you comfortable I've bought some good food we'll eat well tonight hope You like chicken if not I've got fish and plenty of salad. With fries of course and I have thought about What we could do we'll stay in and listen to a collection of naturist music I've collected them for Years". "I've been watching the sun it's a good view from here you must like it here

I've just seen something stranger that thought it might have something to do with the vision in The park the one with the hood seems to have a friend or others should we say hooded seer's of the Paranormal. Nothing to do with us not as far as I know never mind let's just wait then the story will Really take of, what are we doing tonight we could go out if you want to".

We will stay in I feel comfortable here. Do you want to call anyone or use the computer? Internet. York was a quiet place to be the park could be seen sitting they talked of the times they enjoyed while living in York. Jacob kept the food secret and hoped she liked what he described she glanced and he waited she said she smelt meat she was hungry and drank wine little but laughed at here passion.

Jacob asked her questions he was becoming very suspicious but she admitted she had a very important family and she didn't even know where they worked. Jacob explained that his grandfather was a scientist and liked astronomy and space travel. Saying he gave him the apartment and furnishings. He showed Virtue pictures of his inventions virtue smiled she was telling Jacob lies he knew but somehow had to sneak his words as if to say?

Virtue sat comforting the cushions she looked glorious Jacob took well to her she constantly touched his hand saintly food was needed he spoke and cooked stroganoff and rice with a fresh milkshake with real fruit he walked and asked of choosing music she was drinking too mush wine passing coffee remarks she drank three coffees and ate cheese snacks and a few chocolate biscuits.

He had almost finished Virtue explained that her father used to know his grandfather. He stopped and sat she smoked and explained who her father was she said that he was a undercover government worker and didn't have a name to speak of she didn't know what he did but he was a genius and was concealed from any public members his name wasn't known to her. Jacob finished cooking they sat near the window. Smiling she ate considering her appetites.

Listening to Jacob was thankful while he was excited he didn't give virtue much chance she listened apparently the family was connected in some way and it wasn't known they spoke of other family but their was no ties.

Washing up and settling to a beer Jacob redressed and showered virtue prepared her room. She laid grinning at secrets of airs she would have to explain that she was unknown to Jacob and his future was beheld by unknown forces family indeed a brilliant father and a unknown mother and she was a virgin carrying a child of unknown entrance. Sitting she walked sitting in a favourite she knew home and store at the famous park where her father once lived it this very apartment where he discovered a little boy who wrote a book guessing thought she caressed her blond hair brushed by warm sunshine airs.

Jacob freshened they sat separate and little converse made silence thinking about his encounter with Noah he wrote notes of his story 'Animal Bible' he worked listening to music the sun was lowering he felt the atmosphere she smelt of feminine instinct he began to realize she was pregnant and was trying to relate.

He had never seen a pregnant woman virtue was young Jacob was thirty two virtue was twenty-nine and quite short she held good posture she could of dance when she was younger just another question.

They admired the lowering of the sun the river glimmer red colours the curtains were closed. Virtue was tired and needed to shower Jacob pointed everything out. She dressed after in one of Jacobs robes they were cotton and used by guests his mother made them years in the cupboard they remained until.

Sitting watching the room they spoke of comforting their minds the quite was blessed Jacob tensed Virtue calm him he spoke of his unknowing of child saying he could hear the Child's heartbeats holding her hand he sat still the Sun disappeared he began to sweat and washed twice Virtue sat and asked for little foods Jacob helped her speak her mind. He didn't want to ask of the fatherhood. She sleepily spoke of his presence in the apartment.

The rooms grew warm Jacob suggested playing games then asked her Child's name he said he would guide her to inner truth and Virtue spoke of seeing her future husband. She didn't know what happened she felt sick and hungry her doctor told her she was pregnant she said she felt at one and decided she should leave her abode she had walked in the streets for two nights.

Jacob asked if she knew him she said very little and asked why she was pregnant Jacob drank and slumbered words saying it wasn't him. And being confused by his vision of Noah didn't know anything but an obvious night of sex.

Virtue smiled asking if he was the child. She shook and drank her eyes were tired and she brushed her eyes of hair sleeping on Jacobs shoulder he walked her to her room. She undressed Jacob folded the robe he turned off the lights. For the awing morning he stumbled to the sitting room to listen to headphone music.

Chapter 3

THE MORNING ROSE SLOWLY Jacob laid sleepy Virtue dressed and wondered the kitchen looking for food and coffee just one cup she compromised. She sang quiet songs and looked out of the window Rowntree garden leapt with light she smiled with wondering eyes the post arrived she picked it up and Jacob greeted her passing the mail she asked of the night.

Jacob wore loose clothing and put his favourite trainers on and drank coffee with chocolate snaps Virtue asked what he would do today. Jacob laughed and said nothing. He was going to run round the park he prepared and left the apartment with music and gave Virtue the controls. She said she could use the computer Jacob walked away he would be back in half an hour.

She sat watching Jacob running through the gardens the pillars and the round trees shone with light he wore plain clothing and waved. She chuckled and tried to wake the morning was bright she slept very little she decided to go back to bed.

Jacob ran his usual distance saying hello as usual it was dry and moist the mist had cleared people were walking as they always did. Jacob shivered and smiled today he thought about yesterday he hadn't quiet realized but his future laid in hands and he ran back to the apartment Virtue would be awaiting.

Jacob Greek he thought breathing at the door open as usual he entered virtue was on her bed he smiled he turned on the shower and made a black coffee. He sat lazily gazed contemplating he had questions a little music played he smiled trying not to laugh. Today was always the same the gardens roared in sunlight he held his posture his legs moist with water cooling he wore a perfect smile with tired eyes he drank.

The park was busy a gathering had begun many people playing music and chanting they wore colour clothing arranging themselves in the middle of the park. People passed Jacob sat in the window looking Virtue wandered the flat trying to settle Jacob asked her to sit he hugged her ushering words.

She tried to move but he suggested he gave her a robe that his mother used to wear. It was silk and cotton. She said no until he told her to undress she smiled and sat next to him drinking fruit.

Jacob spoke. Asking Virtue what her grandfathers name was she replied and said that he was a farmer in Greece he was very poor and his grandson brought great fortune she said that he died and nobody saw him again. Jacob quizzed and asked if she had seen her family and confirmed the pregnancy. She said no and asked him to wait. Virtue said her father would be at the door within the next few days.

Time passed they aimlessly thought Jacob found her motherly spirit difficult she had never had child she didn't know how to behave sitting he leant to speak to her as he hardly knew himself he almost mastered the art of baby communication she showered everyday Jacob pampered her giving gifts she called him names and wished to be alone. He pretended to be busy and left the apartment for hours then she needed him to be present.

The baby had to wait they were starting to question the appearance of the conception she found it difficult to understand she didn't tell Jacob but her father had called they arrived at his door at five O clock in the morning Jacob was placed in his seat they spoke in foreign languages and her father sat staring at Jacob. Speaking he gestured. They wore suits and watched. Virtue entered calling to her father cussed.

Chapter 4

ER FATHER MADE EXCUSES AND couldn't settle she slapped him and sat he waved his arms and spoke of his presence. She sat and listened he asked her what she was doing. She reminded him of who Jacob was. He stopped and sat. I understand he said. She sat quietly and decided to dress. The cloud bore white light of rays Jacob was asked to remain seated they made coffee.

Virtues father smiled he took off his jacket and asked for a cigarette Jacob asked a question her father put his finger to lips saying "Not yet"?

Jacob sat quietly deciding to make coffee he walked looking at his personnel bodyguards he shrugged and hummed a tune. Virtue entered the sitting room she shouted and screamed her father sat staring at her he was furious. She calmed she sat Jacob was told to sit.

He listened she was told to explain herself they spoke in Greek he couldn't understand he wanted to leave her father told him to sit in his bedroom and smoke. He resisted but was refrained.

He sat on the veranda and drank lager smirking, Virtue calmed and spoke to her father his assistance waited outside. She spoke to Jacob insisting that he knew her father kept refraining her Jacob was confused and explained they sat and spoke of how they met.

They stumbled over words Jacob asked her father looked sternly he was angry he asked him "How she pregnant"? Jacob shivered he sat quietly and waited.

Her father was intense he took a cigarette and gazed asking her how she was pregnant and Virtue replied 'She didn't know' her father swore at her and stormed the room shouting he held her shoulder speaking in Greek. Then he kissed her holding her cheek he looked at Jacob wished him farewell. He left Jacob didn't move he sat watching them leave he looked from the back of the apartment. He thought.

Virtue sat slightly shivering she asked for a coffee speaking to herself she held her dress pulling Jacob sat and spoke she didn't know what was on her mind Jacob tidied up and put music on Virtue calmed.

They spoke for an hour Virtues father had wished the father of the child dead. Jacob was fearful. She insisted that it wasn't them and sat explaining that he wasn't what Jacob knew. He hid everything. She said she would wait. She wanted to go to a church and speak to a priest. Jacob took her it was only a walk in to town. York city. The minster waited. They walked the rowntree garden.

Jacob drove virtue to a church she quickly walked to the door. Their was no presence Jacob said they should try the side door. She quickly panicked the door was open they walked in the church was empty Jacob stood allowing her to enter she called to the outer and sat on a seat.

Jacob sat on other seat and looked at the alter. She started crying and quickly looked around a young female entered she stood and watched the alter Virtue rose.

Virtue asked her where the priest was she pointed and she walked she met the priest who welcomed her she sat with him and he held her hands calming. He listened Jacob sat distanced listening to the airs. Virtue explained her situation.

The priest said that the had never crossed a virgin and was wishing she was blessed he told her to speak the truth and do not hide yourself from yourself,

The priest wanted to see Jacob they spoke and yet Virtue was frightened the priest ensured her she was welcome to stay in the church quarters any time she wished. She agreed and asks Jacob. Jacob store and said he would leave.

Virtue kissed him and spoke about her father. Jacob sat and watched the priest walk with her to her quarters. Jacob prepared to buy clothes and garments. He stood and walked to the car he parked in York city with money he bought gifts as Virtue had asked.

York was busy he hurried and stopped to have coffee sitting with clothes he smoked and left he walked to the car. He calmed he wasn't sure what was happening he wanted Virtue to stay with him trying to think he arrived at the church.

Chapter 5

A HUGE PARK AND VIRTUE HAD spoken of her grandparents owning one. Jacob viewed the matters her father was a underworld worker of Earth she stressed that he did not mention to him yet he seemed so righteous and Jacob didn't like him at all in fact he loathed the sight of him he drank lager and closed the blinds the night was closed he listened to music and slept.

Awaking Jacob noticed the quiet airs he sat and looked at his mobile phone he considered ringing his dad in fact he needed to. He lazed in the sitting room considering making calls. He showered and spoke to himself. Notting he listened to music and danced he didn't know what to do.

The night was near he thought. He called his Dad. Jay was in mind he called his dad and spoke of meeting him within the days. He agreed his Dad was surprised and spoke to Jacob he was quite distressed and uncertain.

Accob; Jacobs father arranged to meet when thought he would arrive in his small car. He would walk the flat to which he always did smelling the air he assumed and spoke thought. Virtue was the figure Jacob tired and said little. Accob was weary and fixative. Jacob insisted that he wasn't the father and made more coffee.

Accob would ask question. Endlessly he was concerned and asked about Virtues father. Jacob was in two minds as if he felt endangered.

Accob sat and said Jacob, he would ask questions. His Grandfather was dead and all his paperwork was in the loft. He self said; he would look for names and information regarding Virtue. He was lying and yet Jacob knew he smiled the bathroom door closed. Settling he grinned he knew their was conspiracy.

Jacob invited a friend he spoke on his phone he called him and suggested he bring wine lots of wine Jacob prepared pizza also lots of, sat powdered smiling he laughs thought of thought he waited his friend was an artist called Phillo he was oriental and enjoyed his master of Art he was truly a master of dance.

Jacob waited and organized his music. Also he put Black beauty in his TV computer Phillo loved to watch it his tears always cried he would leave with watery eyes.

Jacob was curious and sat calmed the park was empty he put his outer lights of he prepared a bottle of wine his dishes and snacks had been put he was going to ask Phillo questions he was a

Singapore but he was as beheld as you could he was so quick with his mind friendly as the calm sun he always spoke of easily what is suppose to be.

Spoken he would arrive. He was dressed in his clothing he brought the beers and sat expecting to be served. His lord was the apartment.

Chapter 6

H E SANG SONGS AND SOON the door knocked Phillo stood and waited Jacob was fresh he stood and welcomed he greeted and laughed Jacob wasn't quite dressed he changed and wore shorts and a tee-shirt. Sitting he asked Phillo what he had learnt.

Phillo settling said he had been to his Mums house and helped decorate he said he had painted a mural of his Mum in the bedroom his dad said he needed the same mural. Jacob smiled wondering what the picture was Phillo showed him. The picture was projected and Phillo drew round the image. Jacob was impressed. He played music.

Jacob thought about what had happened and tried to explain that he had met Virtue he hesitated and waited Phillo thought he would have a drink he spoke in his unknowing voice he knew something was in the airs Jacob drank his coffee and smoked he was slightly tense. Phillo said the room smelt of females Jacob laughed and admitted he had met Virtue. He wanted to speak about the apparition of Noah.

Jacob sat at ease and explained that he had a hallucination in the park. Phillo sat waiting to speak when Jacob explained that he had met Virtue he stopped and didn't speak. Phillo thought and was quite excited he spoke of his grandfather and said he saw three hallucinations before he died Phillo recognized the signs. Jacob was pleased he opened the wine and drank beer. Phillo wondered why Jacob said Virtue was pregnant.

Phillo spoke quickly and Jacob smiled he seemed to make sense but sidetracked he didn't talk of Virtue as intended he referred to Jacobs premises and felt their was an unknown reason for living here Jacob nodded and then struck.

Virtue is a virgin. Phillo sat quietly turning up the music he danced and asked what Jacob meant. She a virgin she didn't have sex. Phillo sat and thought trying to divert the conversation.

Speaking in thought Jacob explained who she was and that her father was someone he didn't want to know as such. Conversation grew and Jacob settled by calming the atmosphere Phillo had been away and motioned his family.

He had won an award for dance and his partner had obliged to marry him. Jacob took the wine sat and they touched glasses. The pizza was almost ready.

They spoke in the quiet airs the subject was their family connections and the book publishing was laugh. Jacob was loosing track of Virtue. They joked and sat eating food Virtue was surrounded by Nuns and a priest she was leaving soon according to her footsteps she stormed out of the chapel house and walked to Rowntrees Park she had no intention of staying she was half dressed and the police were called.

She was observed entering Jacobs entrance. The door rang Phillo was sleeping and Jacob staggered to the door to see the police and Virtue. A sensitive matter Virtue was allowed in. Jacob was quizzed for ten minuets and settled the night. Phillo was covered and slept with Jet-lag.

Virtue climbed the stair in rags with no shoes Jacob returned and sat he didn't speak Virtue was calm and drank coffee. Jacob looked puzzled and spoke waiting for her reply she store and drank. She sniggered and said the priest was useless she said she didn't sleep a wink.

Phillo woken and slept. They sat quietly Jacob asked her to explain what she was doing. She said she was pregnant and didn't have anything to say. Jacob walked away and went to bed he was empty. She followed him to his room and sat on his bed.

She looked tired he suggested she showered and went to bed. She was playful and said she would talk tomorrow. He laid and spoke the hour then slept. Virtue sat and cried swaying mindlessly speaking to herself. Phillo entered and asked who she was he spoke and left soon after.

The night was quite a night in fact the church known it was obvious. The heavens were rained the priest was questioned the inner mind knew she slept tightly.

Virtue woke early and ate food she had pizza and Mayo with lager. Jacob questioned but didn't flip his words he ate the last and drank coffee. They were confused. Phillo had been sick during the night and wrote a note.

Jacob asked Virtue what happened at the church. She spoke of the nuns and how they constantly pampered her and said prayers she said it was haunting. She left and the clergy didn't know several people saw her walk home. Without question she spoke of the loneliness she was suffering. She spoke "The Child".

Jacob suggested they see a doctor. Virtue mentioned her doctor and Jacob said a garn -ecologist would be ideal. The District hospital would provide a scan and medication to calm her. She nodded saying latter. Virtue asked about visitors and questioned. Jacob had spoken to his father and he would visit soon when he's in England saying he was in the Orients doing business.

Virtue smiled and spoke "Did you know that my father knows yours"? Jacob laughed asking what else she knew. Her father was a nocturnal she stated that his father was an astronomer and studied universes. "My father met his when he passed his university courses the masterly decree: You remember"? Jacob sat with his back straight and store Virtue said that his father specialized in appearance and his doctors had questioned him when he was younger before he became a genius. Jacob had never heard of his mental health in question.

Virtue made coffee and sat she store at Jacobs Cigarette and said that her father was a poor young man who dreamt the University and doctors took him through courses of hell mind-bending studies with observation and dream controls. For a total of fifteen years. In the near end he was arrested for attacking members of staff.

He was in prison for months and a spirit friend spoke to him. It was Jacobs father so said Virtues father but he found out it wasn't. Her father received enlighten that night he heard the Universe and has since the Universals visit him.

Jacob sat holding his head a little tearful. He asked what the reason for all this was. Virtues laugh and crackled. "That's for us to find out: The Child"!

Jacob suggested that they would go for a coffee and ice-cream the weather was perfect, she agreed and they slipped shoes and walked.

The front door was left open people could be heard walking it was Sunday everyone walked with dogs and family. Virtue held Jacobs hand she seemed cold he asked she said Walk.

They walked slowly hand in hand talking of their ventures. Jacob was apprehensive he kept asking about his grandfather. And what they did and since they were buried the time ago. Virtue said they worked together for years and lived solitude lives the unknown hologram world worked in secret even if you tried to mention it would not go further than their mouths.

Jacob asked who is the leading body Virtue walked and said everything that you see in front of you. She mentioned her fathers self awareness and he came home one night he was nearly dead in the morning he fell asleep for days and asked to remain at home.

He recovered she said he was often angry in fact and asked her never to ask what he did for a living. But one day as a child she saw two men outside glowing in the light talking to her father. She drew a picture and still had it in her shoulder bag. " Daddies Light friends" was written on the back.

They ordered coffee and smoked a cigarette sharing. Jacob wanted to find out more and looked around him he shivered slightly and said he needed a meal and offered to buy from a cafeteria coffee and salad with cakes.

They enjoyed ice cream and Virtue said she wanted to see her father one to one. Her father would explain why she was pregnant. Jacob said she could say it was him. Laughing she held his waist and kissed his cheek. Brilliant she claimed with giggles. Perfect muttered Jacob.

Sitting outside the café it was the nearest road to York central they drank coffee and decided that they would travel. They spoke of grave yards and money and visiting their past Jacob insisted they start with his father who seemed innocent they would visit. Jacob said he was a Yorkshire man and lived in a bungalow with his wife since he was a woodworker and enjoyed travelling.

Virtue asked questions but nothing was relative to his grandfather. He was buried in York city they walked to Full ford cemetery and looked. They found his grave. They studied the family. And decided to use the computer to find relatives. They walked home Virtue was uncomfortable and needed water Jacob tended to her needs and bought her a pizza sharing it warmed her inners.

She tried to smile asking what she would do. Jacob reassured her spoken of her child. You know me not the child she smiled.

Chapter 7

T HEY RETURNED HOME AND JACOB called Phillo. He considered Jay his brother but he was busy.

Jay was also in questions Jacob knew he was brilliant and Jacob very rarely saw him he dismissed notion and spoke to his father Jacob would visit his father within the hours. He spoke unsure of words Jacob said he needed to ask questions they would have a meal in a pub in Stanford Bridge the swordsman pub tomorrow at one O clock. Jacob agreed.

Virtue was being sick Jacob had ices in the freezers and she ate the most and was sick again Jacob played music to which Phillo bought for him. It was very harmonizing typically oriental. Humming in the background.

Jacob looked at family names and found what he wanted. Then he looked and history and pictures of their families. He kept looking Virtue was asleep Jacob smoked in his dressing-down and drank very bitter coffee smiling he laughed. Speaking to himself "Its Brilliant"!

Jacob asked himself about Virtues virgin pregnancy and quizzed her fathers dream state as he was experimented on sitting he asked Phillo if he could find computer programs related to Virtues father and speaking he said it was too difficult laughing he spoke "Your brother knows".

Jacob listened to music and Virtue had showered sitting in her room she had grown attracted to a soft rocking chair she gazed at the lowering sun Jacob was asked to leave her alone. She played with her phone saying her father had answered and would be visiting.

Phillo had noted the dream factors and entered virtues details their seemed to be names that compared it all seemed to be American he said the experiments were war related but one sight connected with hologram experiences. Jacob looked and saved the files erased he sat looking at profiles a warning appeared and Phillo closed it.

The dream programs were their but it was defiantly hidden Jacob asked Phillo not to mention it they talked of Jacobs brother and Phillo slept on the sofa.

The house in the park had silenced Jacob was excited yet a little disturbed he knew it was what he didn't know. Awaiting the morning became.

They ate in the morning waiting for people to pass with open windows and warming air they sat to see the park Jacob dressed soon and went running he ran the full three miles and sat eating a hot dog drinking his water the river was calm he sat by the stream dipping his hands it would be warm today.

He considered his father calling he had his phone they talked he would be arriving today at one O clock he thanked him and had not told him anything saying it was important.

He walked home Virtue had left the apartment and left a note she had gone shopping again Jacob told her to borrow money at any time she had been shopping three times junk and more junk he threw most of it away she was becoming lazy he would talk to her.

Jay had left a message and asked Jacob to ring. He did so and spoke to Jay was unsettled and made excuses and yet sounded angry he asked who Virtue was and accused Jacob of lying Jacob quickly hung up Jay was in Canada and would be back in England in three days they had arranged a date. They didn't speak therein after.

Chapter 8

ACOB PREPARED FOR THE MEETING she was shopping for clothes and he noticed how much she had taken. He had plenty of money quite where it came from he didn't know but held his chin he was excited to meet his father.

He walked in the apartment and Jacob sat calming the airs Jacobs father sat Jacob asked questions and his father didn't answer all but waited Jacob asked if he knew Virtues father he shook his head and waved his hand Jacob showed him pictures. He looked and said he had seen him but not by name he met him in Switzerland at the airport he was with a medical officer and was arrested.

Jacob asked again Jacobs father spoke I was being questioned by authorities and he passed saying it was years ago he was in the news papers a question of apparent he was convicted but arrested for attempting to enter information in a computer he tried to dress as another person he was detained and sent back to America the news was he was placed in mental institution.

Jacob explained that he was Virtues father and he was a dreamer and put in state one which meant he was in section one dreams. Yes said Jacobs father he was programmer and nearly killed. The FBI took his computer he said he was put in prison. He left two months after, after his case was thrown out of court they said he was a qualified Doctor and he wasn't at all. He claimed he controlled Hologram Universes.

Jacob laughed asking why he knew he said he gave him a cigarette and the police asked questions. He said they wore unusual uniforms they were dotted in the airport. Jacob asked what else he knew his dad said he died according to the news papers.

He died of "stricken one"; in a dream state. Jacob mentioned the computer research and pictures he told his father he had seen him he was still alive. His father spoke unsure asking if he had been to see Virtue Jacob said yes with his bodyguard.

Virtue returned and Jacobs father smiled thinking she was cute she took his hands nodding she put her bags down showing Jacob baby clothes and dummies with food Jacob put everything away. Virtue smiled Jacobs father asked her questions about the baby? She spoke calmly and said she would know soon the baby would be born soon.

They spoke of Doctors she said all was clear. Jacob walked and mentioned Jay saying he couldn't make it to see him. Jacob asked his dad what he did he said he was an officer for an unknown Canadian company involved with computers.

Chapter 9

JACOBS FATHER SPOKE OF HIS confusing youth and said he spoke of visions and where he was from. He also spoke of his grandfather saying his mother was not seen. He was adopted and never really knew himself. Jac Jacobs father said he appeared at the door of the farm where his father lived and begged for food.

He entered the farm house three times and he worked always confused and tired Jacs father took pity he checked the villages and no one knew him.

He earn a good name he became a icon for the animals he seemed to have healing properties that no one understood he even healed a horse that had bled they said he slept and the horse rose also.

The boy knew he was welcome and spoke of a strange man in a garment he woke and he was in a barn he pointed outside and cried. Jac laughed and shook his head he never believed him but found out it was true the cloths were given to him by spirit as the boy claimed.

The boy said he didn't have a name and said his friend the goat was called Jay. He asked who the goat was and the boy said it died. The boy was asked questions otherwise he didn't know anything and spoke of a man with many spirits.

Jac brought the boy up and taught him discipline and honour he was very fierce and calmed. His anger was present in his eyes Jac didn't like it but one day a Sheppard appeared and he taught him sports. Running and fighting with the stick. Jay learnt over the years and never feared again. He never entered the barn. Often he cried and walked away.

One day the Sheppard arrived at the door and took Jay on a short journey to the Greek temples and woodlands. They travelled by foot. Jay was given two hours to find a stick. The Sheppard sat and prepared food. Jay walked and found four and five trees.

He walked back and ate. They went to the trees Jay claimed he had seen the same trees Anod the Sheppard laughed and said point. Then he said walk. Jay stopped Anod asked which branch. He passed a saw and sat down.

Jay climbed the tree and cut. He was scratched and bloody the stick fell to the floor. Anod looked and said we must go back. The whole branch was heavy and jay dragged it half a mile he complained and spoke of his hands. Anod helped with his shoulder they returned to seat and ate bread with milk.

Jay wanted the saw. Anod said they must sleep. He started singing Jay said he wanted to look in the woods. Anod said they would light the fire and sit with a tipple of wine. It sleeps in your eyes. One hour and Anod slept. Rising early in the morning he left Jay under a blanket and went for water and fruit.

Jay rose soon after asking to tend to his stick Anod asked questions about the stick saying he was tall and the stick must be measured. And when he is older can be used as a walking stick. It was for defence Anod had a collection of sticks and practised everyday for years. Anod nodded they had eastern nuts and drank coffee. They cut the stick. Jay was thrilled and watery eyes.

They finished the stick and Anod finished it shaving the outer. Jay was very pleased he danced Anod told him to wait until the bruising had gone.

Jay smiled saying we will fight sticks. Yes we will walk with your stick. Pride he walked he was shacking at first. He settled talking to himself. Singing he kept dancing. Anod walked quickly. The sun grew in the morning. They walked four miles home to the farm.

They were greeted and compromised the journey Jay spoke well and sat with tiring eyes Jac sat and rank orange juice the Sheppard said Jay had been given a gift and at his youth age they would take careful steps to teach him life and defensive discipline to which would keep his intentions to the highest.

Jac thanked Anod they walked to the farm gate speaking of next time Anod smiled as always and walked to the local village where he said he lived. In fact they never really knew where he was from otherwise a person of few secret words.

Chapter 10

HOWEVER JACOB SLUMBERED AND AROSE he panic Virtue sat and smiled she had a tin of beer Jacob sweating and cursed he staggered to the bathroom and redressed. It was due time for sleep. Virtue followed she was caressing him he tried to calm her and kissed her forehead walking away.

She spoke of the child and said that her father had received the edited book that Jacob wrote and New York had been informed. Jacob laughed making coffee. Sniggering she huddled him he shunned and looked at her eyes. She was welling. How was the "Tum Tum" he asked, she sulked and walked behind. O you know how much your worth?

Jacob sat and didn't speak. She played with Jacob he tried not to anger and said twenty thousand? 'My father has earned you one hundred thousand pounds; it is in your account. Check with your computer!

Jacob laughed sitting with music to his ears. Virtue looked giggling. Pointing at the computer. Jacob touched the screen quickly processing he found a credit screen he read a message a complimentary from a book company with his bank details. Total amount One Hundred Thousand pounds. He sat back and closed.

So Virtue, you have a family that you don't know. I'm thinking your father doesn't even know you and you come to me even thought as though. You said you saw me on your dads computer and Noah appears in front of me. I don't know who to accuse of the conspiracy when you are the one that chose?

My Father is nothing to do with it, I read your profile a farmers boy with no money and a very rich grandfather who gave you this house and park. The wills are waiting you have to ask your father this house and park belongs to you.

I'm not quite sure what your saying but I own half of it the park owns the rest. It belongs to you virtues eyes glance at the computer.

Would you like to see the will and testimonies. Jacob stubbed and starred at her pointing she rose and entered her web site. Here she smiled and he looked. He controlled the computer virtue assisted.

She spoke "Its simple" your grandfather said ask your father. The last words have stated the park belongs to you. The designs are on the other pages. Ill show you' theirs the pictures its your grandfathers designs, for you to complete. Virtue spoke and walked to her room singing a song. Goodnight 'Greek'.

Jacob sat imposed he thought of Yorkshire as a place he remained in self of self. Kindly thinking of his ownership he graced the park with eyes. Rowntree waterfalls sports birds and the river would be clear of view.

Chapter 11

WHILE HE SAT HE WANTED to assume the visiting of Switzerland to visit his grandparent grave. Virtues grandfather also. He booked an appointment outside their was a voice calling then many it was late Jacob booked the flight and sat checked of his account he arranged his mind with held views of the Park in York city.

He grew tired and thought of the wills of his grandfather Virtue said they were on the computer and needed to be identified and send to his new address. He thought till he laid sleeping the garden of gardens. Rowntrees he smirked the night was black with closed eyes the sofa felt so perfect he rose very slowly risen virtue played music looking at the river.

Jacob rose looking at the window breathing he watched virtue sat in the sun light fiddling with her hair. He groaned and barely spoke virtue glanced and drank her coffee he spoke she crossed her legs. 'Your breakfast is cooked. Jacob doubled over staggering to the bathroom.

Jacob was confused he had booked to go to Switzerland to see two ghosts he had one hundred thousand pounds half of his family were all hologram he owned rowntree park and he was static. He grinned in the mirror.

The baby was in the time of Jacob was aware and couldn't quite reassure himself. Virtue was full of spirit and convinced Jacob to bow down he was nerves and utterly calmed he kept his words and carried on the usual of the day. Speaking to Virtue was small words until mentioned the baby and bedroom she enlightened smiling. Self control was a obligation to self thought.

They had organized their bags for the three days they would spend in Switzerland sitting talking of addresses and places to visit. Virtue said her father had organized a car with driver he would arrange the journeys to see the Tombs and the visits to family her father had organized the visit.

Jacob sat to attention and drank coke he kept looking at Virtue she wanted food and kept complaining Jacob spoke and they left the apartment the post master walked pass they walked by the river Jacob spoke of the park and with total demand the day was long and prolonged he wanted to create sheer brilliance virtue called his nature and played with childlike words it annoyed him.

Sitting they kissed cheeks virtue held his hand she confirmed that she had been cleared by the doctors and was ready then she read minds speaking of what she knew of Jacob he shivered and said no putting his finger on his lips saying enough. She wiped her eyes. He laughed "Are you a ghost". She held his shoulder.

Jacob thought of hologram universes and wished he knew more he didn't ask and yet he was very wary? He hadn't met a universal and was slightly precautions he looked at the sun.

Then Jacob suggested they go to baby classes to which he had organized they would spend one hour of baby talk and virtues insides nothing thought. Jacob they left and smiled walking back home she was pleased he waited for the next clue.

Walking back they noticed police and turned away Jacob was aware that they felt conspicuous and the laughed at the opportunities of being addressed.

They held view and the park returned to view they spoke of Switzerland and prepared when they returned home Virtue sat and organized everything with fingers and words she mastered the art of arts and he stood with stars around listening to music he stood and growled. He feet edged and Virtue made him more coffee.

It took three hours the telephone rang and friends were asking. Virtue turned them away saying they were preparing for their holiday. Virtue also became tired and laid on the sofa. She had ordered a baby comfy seat specially designed in France. It was due soon Jacob stripped to the waist and took his slippers off.

Sitting with the warmth of freshet air began Virtue was crying Jacob sat and store they spoke and ushered words he spoke of food she said no food but ate ice creams and strawberries. Jacob sat on the veranda.

The emails had been answered and no invites were made Virtue had fallen to sleep and covered Jacob looked at Virtues email and messages. He grew very conscious and quickly glanced.

He read most of her messages and quietly closed he knew who she was but the people she wrote to didn't know her it seemed. Her father clenched the airs he was awaken and fell silent. He bathed and dimmed the candle lights.

Jacob sat and played with fingers he hadn't written for a long time he was writing the play Animal Bible finishing was easy his eyes glanced the screen watching Virtue she was three months pregnant and contemplation was becoming too much Jacob sat with paper and a smile nearly finished?

The morning was risen Virtue asked what he was doing on the sofa Jacob made crispiest and sat and sniggered the baby was doing him in. He said the doctor told you "Your having a baby"! She walked slowly to the bathroom and asked for Jacob. He shouted 'no' scratch your own back.

Chapter 12

WALKING WAS EASY WHEN LIFE forms controlled you she complained and spoke of Switzerland saying her father would call. He did and he arranged the time four hours it seemed to be. Jacob stood in the window and they waited for a car. Three cars ten security men and two dogs.

Smiling he hugged Virtue speaking ushering his eyes welled asking what the baby was going to be called she grabbed his arms saying 'Noah'. He nodded and wiped his face. 'Why do I know'.

Then standing he showed her the window saying they have been stood there for the last twenty minutes she smiled she said the holograms appeared at needed times she recognised one of them pointing.

Virtue looked at the clouds she said that whispering cloud meant 'Animal' was near and watching Jacob groaned and hugged he asked, she did not speak? 'The Universe is the void'. Jacob asked how she knew Virtue spoke of fear picking her bag Jacob helped they sat and nibbled nails the door bell rang. Jacob waved his keys.

The door was closed Jacob walked with Virtue their future was obvious yet unknown they walked to the gate and a large car awaited two cars in front they wore suits and were armed Virtues father drove behind.

They drove to Full Sutton Village an old airfield awaited. It took three quarters of an hour. Jacob sat Virtues father spoke on the screen.

He showed them a film about their grandparents. It disturbed Jacob but he sat and the film closed. Virtues father smiled and spoke of seeing them their. Speaking of "Happy little one". The air plane was small and sweet within five minutes they were flying above. Sleep was arranged they sat looking at darkness Jacob was sweating he had never flown in a plane.

Jacob slept and mentioned their family drinking he laid awake. Virtue became interested and shivered asking where they were.

First however she mentioned her child her father said that she was pregnant with a tablet and her father spoke of the doctors. Apparently everyone was involved he had no option.

They flew calmly Jacob was sweating and wanted to drink the nurse tended giving him drinks and a sedative he sat and threw up three times saying it was the last time he would fly. Virtue sat smiling watching her fathers videos become cunning she realized that her father was who he was and she couldn't hold back.

Her father explained she was the beginning of an end Noah had become too old and wise the entity of Universe had called he required to be human 'You were chosen' sat calmly she asked her father to kiss her he hugged and said wait and see your grand parents they know everything about the future and past.

They flew for hours and Jacob sat looking white and tense Virtue ate food and the Sun called they sat and nearly landed. It was a good flight and the staff had been arranged a limo with helicopter aerial view. They walked and sat her father sat in the same car.

Three cars imposed in the first sunlight they timed everything they would travel five miles they sat and silence prevailed Jacob smiled with quick statements to himself and virtue he spoke of feeling death and opened the window all little too much.

The helicopter hovered in the distance the quiet road became quiet distanced in the distance a crowd was being observed they were told not to worry it was a group of supporters they had heard of Noah and rebirth they drove slowly two or three hundred people had gathered the police tended to their needs flashing lights and voices were heard Virtues father smiled saying 'We will see them again' he held Virtues hand.

Virtue asked him what was happening he explained that the spoken words of her child had been passed and she was blessed the human nation and world had been confirmed millions knew and yet would gather. 'They are pleased' We must protect ourselves and the child Noah he is a blessed child of unbelievable proportions and must handed the book of 'Animal' to which he will follow.

Virtue cried and held hands Jacob sat still and they soon arrived in a small village to hence they stopped the police had arrived and they asked people had gathered at the door of a small house behind a grave yard. They waited the police cleared the area they drove slowly and parked.

Chapter 13

H E ORDERED THE GUARDS TO stand ground they walked to the doors they opened candles shone Jacob asked for coffee. Virtue sighed and stood she had been here before and froze. A servant tended. Speaking in slight English. Old and gracious she bowed eyes.

She spoke 'Little Virtue I remember you; follow me' Virtue smiled walking she laughed slowly she was old and bearable she crackled walking pointing at pictures telling of Virtues family she stopped and smiled 'That is you your grandfather painted it' Virtue stopped and asked for a coffee. Virtue asked how old the picture was she walked and fetched the picture she wrapped it. 'He want you to keep it' Virtue was taken she said put in pocket.

Virtue looked in the gardens smiling the old woman asked to walk. They sat the coffee was brilliant and little soft butter biscuits sitting the old lady smoked a cigarette and crackled laughing .You have a child other know you and you have a puff.

The old lady spoke of her husbands and pulled a bottle of spirits from her dress. 'You drink' She walked away and pointed at the cigarettes 'You look at heavens'. Virtues father stood in the background Jacob cheeked and kissed her and asked what the hell was going on.

'That lady is so old she's a reincarnate Jacob took a sip and relieved himself finishing his coffee. He asked what they were going to do. Virtue said that the Yeti Tombs were here and they had to wait.

Her father asked for her she walked in the Sunlight eyes glimmering he said they were to go to the burial ground first then to see her grand parents just a walk away. She nodded and asked for Jacob. They walked.

Standing in the garden grounds Virtues father pointed in one direction. The walked to the bottom of the garden and walked through trees small trees hundreds of then and stopped. The trees circled they stood and an old man with a stick prodded the ground and smiled the house owner walked first he walked thought a barrier and stood Virtue's father asked them to follow.

Jacob stopped and watched Jacob watched a Tomb appear their wasn't yet a door. The old man disappeared inside. It was physical and the aroma smelt the airs. Jacob asked where the burial ground was. They explained that there was only one place all the bodied were in once place. He explained that the Tomb master was a reincarnate and they had been here after death.

Virtue smiled and asked where their grandfathers were. Virtues father spoke of a house beyond the trees. It was five minutes away and they were waiting. Virtue touched the tomb rock walls feeling electric she jumped and walked away.

They stood and looked at the tomb the entrance was underneath it was closed and sealed the heavens were blue told by gardener today was a good day to see the untruth many had seen and unknowing spoke many thought their was a tomb but in truth their wasn't anything the ground was empty.

However the ground memory was recorded and persons had spoken of appearing of request the dead had appeared and dreams were noted many people asked but denied the quest of knowledge the government had asked and turned away from reality to facts.

Nothing existed in ground hologram no records found only a doctors file who died of insanity. He in fact died of many names and lives today. Virtue smiled and laugh asking where her grandfather was. "Little trees" "Little trees"!

They walked Virtue held Jacobs hand through trees to a field of small trees that were hundreds of years old thousands of years old twisting and entwined spoken of warm and loved ones gnarled by characters posit held as airs of bark. They stood watching birds fluttered and sang.

The house master spoke of a tree pointing he called a door opened a hologram house appeared wooden and perfect in construction roof of tree wood and leaves grown by thousands of years of pruning they stood and the door opened they entered the inner garden entry was watered with flowing water fresh moist airs and warmth in distance.

The servants appeared and guided Virtue to the opening she held her mouth spoken of few words she could hear birds and two dogs appeared panting at her feet. They stood to attention and sat staring at her.

The servants tended to Virtue taking her hands they guided her walking slowly the dogs walked away she looked at the trees and inner garden furnishing would be placed the walls of entwined wood covered her steps she walked the servants stopped and told her to sit.

They sat and waited water was served coffee and incense sticks were offered they a old man appeared dancing in the airs he spoke of Virtue and her child he laughed and shivered speaking hysterically Virtue looked around the sun shone through the ceiling she held Jacobs hands servant walked past smiling.

The old man said they were to be greeted and walked away. Two other old men entered in distance they wore light clothing and slowly walked. They looked old and enabled speaking they held their hands to Virtue asking of the child. Touching Virtue asked who was who?

"We are your grandfathers" She stood and hugged taking care not to misjudge she held his hands you're my grandfathers?

"Yes" and you are Virtue and Jacob. He tended to Jacob holding his hand he shook it and crackled saying he was last person he expected asking him to sit. The grandfather's sat with cigars and coffee spoke well for their child.

The old eccentric man was excited "He little Noah" You must realize they quickly spoke of the future and silenced.

You have a child that brings truth to our destiny the future lies in the creation that Jacob wrote the spirit of Noah lies in you. You are the gifted one the child Universe brings great future to Animals he will nature as a child and will see the greatness of Kingdom the voids will see in time. Both grandparents spoke over he bent over and held her hands Yes he is the child I hear laughter and trembles.

Virtue sat and was offered drinks she chose hot nut honey and tree sap water with burnt cinder the eccentric old man laughs it is the drink we will watch the child become he very thirsty!

The grand parents spoke of Jacob speaking of minds in ways playful of details Jacob asked their names they smiled and pointed at each other. "Jaka" is my name he pointed at the twin laughing the twins said their names were the same and always had been. "Mother thought well to be twins"? "Jaka and Jaka's.

"You're older than me" I can't remember you're the same twin I've always known we agreed we should keep the difference to our selves so Mother told. Jacob sat and smoked the house hologram was fantastic the twins spoke of the wooden ceiling "It never rains only when the twine grew now it is always Suns. The Universe always watches the Kingdom. The dead pass always the Universes are never seen they are always present.

There is presence in the house of little trees the unseen is a void of OM the entrance of the hologram is total in the exact excisable Universe you cannot change it all forms in memory the touch of the quiet beyond anyone's imagination but perfect to all that touch the entrance of Universe.

The twins spoke of child muttering quietly of the OM and the music of within. They spoke of Virtue and spirit. Jaka spoke of her inner state and the age of her appearing self spoke of music she would hear. "Your beyond will disturb you and you must calm, sit when you see eyes of brightness and listen to the music it is the OM calamity is otherwise and you will listen "Sing my child Sing".

Its is also the darkness of the Voids the bearing cannot see beyond yet the eyes of dream wakening is not of little Noah it is he sees as he has.

Jacob sat the twins looked as he shivered. One twin spoke of the ghost. Then laughed ordering wine. Virtues father sat and drank with laugh Jacob walked and looked in one place of the door.

The twins held eyes with virtue assuring her of Jacob. He was concerned and confused little of his capable mind walking he passed twine doors looking at the ground fearing the presence. Clothes were placed and the aroma lingered he touched and tended to seats he sat and store.

Emptiness seemed to dwell breathing heavily he noticed a dry book picking it up he noticed the language of the book. Letters and symbols he played with the sand on the floor.

Drawing the pictures he laughed shouting called his name he rose and carried the book. It was "Twine Verse"

He walked the twins were drinking and music could be heard. Jacob raised his hand before he could speak. The elder servant friend touched his arm. She waved her finger she passed Jacob water waiting for Jacobs response.

Jacob tried to step the servant lit a cigarette and passed to him. She pointed at the seat she walked him to. Jacob didn't realize that the book had disappeared. She spoke clearly and crisply "Sit and do not speak above other". Jacob had calmed and store the servant pointed at the coffee and left the cigarettes a twine oil lamp was in front on a table of twine.

The lamp was made of twine roots a small flame Jacob flickered the flames and smoked he glanced the twins were drinking Jacob sniggered their eccentric behaviour amused him.

Virtue looked tired and wanted to walk in the inner grounds she stood and held Jacob by the hand the twins carried on talking. She wiped her eyes and pointed in the distance they walked the water fountains were in front the upper levels were seen Sun light exposed the distance rooms.

Virtue spoke of the house and felt calm Jacob asked what to do next. Virtue said the Kingdom of Animals were outside and always waited. Lost souls Virtue laughed "NO" the Universe has given them full view they can be anywhere at any time it's a gift! Jacob spoke what will the Holograms do? "They all become one"!

How many animals was a question they sat and watched the night fall intending to stay for the weeks they relaxed in a chamber it fell near a slight Cliff the Sun lowered they unpacked and laid on the bed Virtue cried out that the twine airs smelt beautiful and the veils caressed her body.

Breathing she held views. The night grew dark while virtue walked the rooms grew darker the shade of lights became accustomed she quickly glanced the airs were smelt the gardens appeared in distance with water.

In most rooms sprinklings of moisture food could be smelt she sat and waited for attention her father spoke earlier and stressed that she must be alone she contemplated the child Noah was considered she was calm and spirited a little too enlighten.

Pillars of twine wooden wood held the ground of rock and soils listening to her heart beats Virtue spoke to herself ushering little musical tunes words she had never heard from her material state of mind she cried her emotions held by her eyes sitting on a seat of comforting cotton she breathed heavenly with her head back watching the insects flying the few their were.

Virtue could sense the OM the Universe held her eyes she was scared and the door was in the distanced eyes she couldn't figure her inners turning to her son Noah she calmed she heard voices and gatherings of music she stood a servant walked behind her lights began to appear calls were in the airs of night.

Chapter 14

THE POLICE WERE CALLED THEY surrounded the house waiting for assistance people had gathered in there hundreds the sky for dark and stars shone Virtue was guided to a safe place to sit Jacob looked through the windows he was amazed thousands of people had gathered the field were candle lit they sang and danced he could hear the songs.

Virtue calmed him she spoke of the child and massaged her body Jacob wasn't quite sure what to do he walked the bedchamber looking a helicopter covered the sky then he saw cameras it was no time for media.

Virtue asked for the doctors she said she was frightened a servant came to their room and game her a drink of 'Soothe'. A medical drink to clear her airways and two biscuits of wheat.

Everyone had to gather in the main room they were all confused the twins remained in their quarters and apparently walked the field due to eccentrics'.

Virtue decided to allow the media in and spoke to them regarding the event. The crowds were fighting to see her on the front doorstep. Virtues father spoke to the media then virtue said a few words. Speaking the crowd roared virtue stopped and walked away.

The night grew everyone had quietened the police had calmed and remained at all doors a few armed offices remained in observe and controlled the crowd. The thousands waited till morning this was the night of calling.

Noah and the realm of universes had appeared the world in the morning would be changed the woke to see!

Settle the airs became warm and humid Jacob laid with virtue they smiled at fortune creating their inner peace keeping the air breathable Jacob was aware now he realized and couldn't hold his inspiring revelations disbelief left him he held his eyes resting.

The morning rose little light the window was gazed Jacob looked the gathering had lessened he looked drinking coffee Virtue was asleep Jacob didn't leave the room. Virtues father tended to her needs another man also Jacob walked besides.

They descended the stairs entering the centre house Jacob smiled speaking of the quiet airs he sat with coffee and smoked a pipe he didn't know what it was a servant smiled after lighting it puffing he grinned and Virtue stood her aroma glowed he bowed his head looking at the twine house he could hear the water tricking from and too.

Virtue was held by her thought standing still she held her hands dancing with realm she smiled she was aware of herself she was heavenly pregnant and wanted to consume her self thought a little boy walk through a door he was a perfect image he stood in front of Virtue smiling touching her hands she smiled he held both of her hands he then walked behind speaking in his own words.

Virtue asked quietly who he was her servant said he is only one spirit 'They appear in hologram always'. Virtue shivered and gazed at Jacob. He stood and walked towards the entrance front of house he wanted to leave Virtues father exclaimed ,'We are to leave'?

They gathered outside the door of house people were talking to each other cameras watched every move they made shouting gave unsightly airs they sat in a limousine and drove to the airport it took a short time drinking coffee they discussed their over night stay, it all happened so quickly.

Virtue store outside what she saw was the fields with the Sun shone millions of faces wavered past her eyes disappearing in amidst she spoke of inner child she was nearly ready she held hands.

Virtue's father observed every notion of herself she asked him to be observant otherwise she didn't speak about his experience he very rarely spoke of the experiments that had been practised while he became 'Holo' as he said.

She noticed that he changed his voice and his eyes changed colour he was a trained martial artist for many years then he taught himself dance as he would say. Sitting he played with his hands he would often dance moving with thought he knew himself otherwise he would shake and turn a ashen colour with strained features.

Virtue knew at later age that Abot her father was terrified she dare not question his mind she spoke kindly and tried to reassure herself Abot left the room again' he was kind but his universe wasn't he didn't know what was expected he wanted to invent Hologram he was told it was forbidden he was an artist that was enough.

They drove in the limousine the distant call of an aeroplane waited for their arrival sitting Jacob sat smiling he had a terrible habit of smiling when no one knew why usually when he drank coffee and smoked cigars 'the little lady gave me cigar', she little lady touching Virtue as breathed the cold airs.

The private airport waited for there entry passes where shown staff waited the door opened they sat the engine started the night held total silence stars glimmered they were welcomed sat in place they were to fly to Full Sutton airfield in England.

The plane roared and lifted in crisp airs of Switzerland leaving, music was played Virtue massaged her belly falling asleep a nurse sat near her seat Jacob watched music Abot stared out of the window with a very fatherly poise.

The birth of Noah was truly apparent the spirit of Universe had taken gladly the self conscious of all in the matter of O.M. Abot bear a grin of how Noah would cope the child was normal he could tell his mother regard was to caress the hair of untouched universe Virtue did not realize.

Jacob was futile he was Greek and knew nothing Virtue had experience every thought of her father he walked in many dead state mind Holo Universe was a brilliance of little light walking with eyes glimmering with all that was the O.M.

They arrived within hours of flying food had been served a movie was aired they sat seeing England excited they strapped up sitting speaking of all but others the guards spoke on their radios the press were present in the small airport.

The computers had reported the gathering of hundreds it was private the airport a closed airport used by wartime persons. They sat Abot spoke to personnel they quickly arranged a place to sit in a car arranged as always.

They landed and the airport could be seen on the ground fires had been lit criss crossing the fields confused they looked Virtue sat and shouted shaking she spoke of fear and the faces of many her nurse sat and gave her calm words she was seeing the air plane parked in the distance the police approached they were armed keeping there distance.

Full Sutton was a small village with an old airport they arrived landing fires were everywhere they could see people running frantic they crazed by the air plane stood still when they landed they stared at the plane hundreds of people holding garments the police were scattered guiding the people to place then they all ran behind the plane.

Jacob stood first he noticed a strange noise outside music was being played it sounded like insects a buzzing hum he panicked and held virtue quickly asking her to stand her nurse told him to stand aside.

Abot spoke to the rest of the people on board reassuring them that they had to keep calm and exit the door to sit in the cars to which had arrived. Quickly they walked the air was clean and cool they looked the crowd gathered most of them sat on the floor waving hands and chanting.

People could be seen in the distance they stampeded towards the air plane they quickly sat in the cars awaiting. The the police guided them safely home as thought they changed the plans and a quiet place would be found. No speech was made on behalf.

Abot stood at the top of the stairs he held his arms high and screeched a piercing sound the crowd stood up and stared murmured then they sang a song Abot thanked them and sat in the car.

Virtue sat in seat and asked what her father had done he said it is called the "ANI" speaking he said it was the call of the dead the animals all know the Ani its always a call of natural instinct it takes years of practice and becomes normal to any one with a dream.

Chapter 15

JACOB SAT AND LISTENED THE police guided the cars to York City the TV was on and news reports were being processed Abot turned it off and calmed Jacob saying it wasn't official Jacob sat and store Abot was reassuring him that Virtue was nearly ready for childbirth and Jacob had to step aside or he would be harmed. Nodding Jacob watched his hand shake with his nerve Abot laughed sitting he played music. This is the "ANI".

They returned to the park friends awaited all gathered and food was before them Phillo was ecstatic Jacob shook his hand spoken hurried words were put to Phillo said that the computers broken and gone crazy three times. Saying I hope you don't mind I bought new computer?

The garden was quiet the river was fresh lights appeared in the distance a helicopter was overhead people spoke strangers seemed to be distanced Virtue was tired and walked to her room Jacob sat with Phillo who insisted he spoke over Jacob store and smiled.

Abot looked around the house pointing out what was in place a giant seat had been placed Phillo tried to explain that it was the mother of Jupiter Gods saying it was delivered by a very large native woman and its a mother child seat for having babies for God sake. Abot touched his shoulder and the wet goat leather seat 'Perfect' Phillo calmed and sat speaking of computers.

Phillo mentioned that the Animal Bible appeared on the computer and a contract had appeared Jacob smiled looking at Phillo they spoke of the contract which needed ID'

And a letter referred to money trying to calm Phillo wiped his forehead. While Phillo had been staying in the flat he spoke of hundreds of people gathering outside all for unknown reasons.

Virtue had washed and took seat near the open widow the sun was rising she was noticeable she couldn't sit still looking at the gift that had been given to her she kept looking at Phillo he drank beer and snoozed he was exhausted.

Smiling she dwelled on inner self Noah was near to and she asked for everything she waited till morning her bedroom had been changed by an unknown African company. Phillo said he was forced to let them in saying they took everything away leaving a round bed with furs and perfect white bedding.

Phillo spoke too quickly Jacob asked him to leave thanking him meanwhile looking around he noticed the gifts were all unwrapped Phillo smiled saying he didn't see one postman!

Phillo walked home quite surprised by the quiet airs sniggering thoughtfully looking at passers by all smiles left his venture in self content almost blissy he kept looking at corners wondrous the Noah had nearly arrived.

He didn't want to be involved yet little of eyes he dwelled with the possibly of knowing the heavens even thou art the animals knew and that was exactly what lingered in the words for windows he didn't want to see the beyond yet awaited.

Chapter 16

THE EXPECTANCY OF BIRTH CLOSED the eyes of Noah sleep of eyes to see the body of Universe will so be and yet parents must oblige in times to await the Birth is as now Virtue waited in comfort speaking of moments she smiled constantly pleased with the huge belly and her countless dishes of small foods.

Virtue rose day of days spoken as quietly she withdrew from her social events sitting in unusual place looking her eyes were bright and crystal she held her belly firmly singing quiet songs Jacob wrote down what she called the songs hoping he would write them down. The night held posture rising the calmed of morning the moon called.

Jacob was called he sat up in bed Virtue groaned and asked what time it was Jacob said six in the morning. He listened to her heart beat holding hand. The mobile phone rang Jacob answered his heart sunk the voice spoke deeply saying "Open the back door your son requires to arrive".

Jacob asked who the voice was the voice said "It is not of you go to the door and remain calm sit in the veranda you will see me you must wait she will call for you hands to hold".

Jacob ran to the back door listening for sound he stopped unlocking the door he put his foot to hold the door he breathed deeply trying to look a midwife spoke quietly ushering she touched his hand behind her were two twin girls standing perfectly still they put their fingers to their lips. The midwife entered the girls followed. Jacob looked one spoke speaking saying "She doesn't know we are present do not mention sit in the window remain quiet" Jacob walked to the bedroom door virtue glanced Jacob knew he had to close the door behind.

The silence was barred Jacob sat drinking water looking outside he noticed glimmers of light in the horizon drinking he strained his ears he looked at the computer the screen was on he thought of emails he smoked counting the ending packet the telephone kept ringing he told himself not to answer.

Shiverish Jacob the door bell rang he stood Virtues father burst in asking questions speaking he noted the phone "You didn't answer" Jacob stammered asking who the children were he laughed "They are Geminious spirits they are present to bring the spirit of Noah to the world he is your sons unseen Twin"

Jacob was taken back slightly angry he snarled asking why he wasn't told? Abot smiled soothing Jacob you have seen Noah once you will see him again tonight, when he is older he will be brought back to you as a family when Noah and Noah's are wise and realize that the world requires to be understand.

He touched his hand 'the entity of Noah is the spirit of all Kingdoms beyond he awaits you sons wisdom of age'. Don't mention until Noah sees his vision even I don't know it will be.

With two names Jacob rest assuring himself he had nothing to speak of sat tense and calmed by the warm air people had gathered outside little music could be heard Jacob looked Abot mentioned that the music was spiritual as wasn't heard by all and humans.

Speaking he spoke of his perceptiveness as aware of eyes he held his hand " close the curtains they see what you cannot".

The light was shaded the midwife spoke calmly speaking of her birth she asked questions Virtue didn't move otherwise she sweated towels were brought Virtue fell asleep she closed her eyes she asked? Who were the hands that held her son?

Calls were made for Jacob shaking with trembles she changed colour and her eyes motioned with rapid grasp she called screaming then she relaxed thinking it was over?

The first child was born the spirit of Noah was present the two Holo girls held the spirit child they dressed standing perfectly still tending with dressing waiting for the second birth Virtue had blacked out the midwife woke her, it was a perfect birth the seat was wet with water Noah followed easily Virtue gasped sleepy holding her arms tended she held.

The Gemini children left crying could be heard Jacob stood the children store at him Abot spoke quietly Jacob looked at the child standing still he held out his hand Abot refrained him saying he must not be touched.

Jacob stood still looking Abot asked him to sit in the window and observe what had happened he shivered muttering walking away he looked again he ran to the back door he saw the girls they entered a Spherical which was blue with 'Holo Earth' written on the outer. Abot closed the door speaking with a firm voice.

Sitting down Jacob stood again he looked at the park gardens voices could be heard Abot said they want to see the child Noah. Jacob looked seeing thousands of faces they spoke in the air breathing could be heard he went silent.

He could be seen the night was dark many stood to attention Abot asked if Jacob could call to the people that the child had been born to make a small speech.

Jacob opened the door and stood they called many spoke cries Jacob raised his hands and shouted that Noah had been born and said he was perfect they could cheered and drums could be heard they began to sit on the grass speaking of the Birth.

The second child was born she called her name Noi spoke a child Holo pleasingly simple moment after holding graces she looked at motherly be love cries of little lips two twins she was half

Holo and she lit the room according to Virtue she shone gazing mother trembled with little shivers.

Jacob shook bowed and turned away he noticed the sky it was so bright he walked asking for a coffee. Virtue sat with a midwife Jacob saw the child he touch him wiping tears Virtue sat in a special seat created by an African tribes man 'as soft as cotton sleeps' Jacob danced eyes and held Noah he smiled the midwife finished their little tasks changing the rooms slightly with soft hands.

Virtue store at Jacob asking for the child speaking of the outside garden Jacob refrained and suggested they speak on behalf of name and to speak in a more suited time.

Sitting together the sound of the park came to chants. They both rose and the midwife held the child for moments. Jacob shouted at first the crowd clapped calming the crowd.

Jacob said in pleasing that the heavens had spoken of little child with the name 'Noah' the crowd didn't make a sound murmuring could be heard. Jacob stood glancing at Virtue she spoke holding the child. The atmosphere called all cries of cries.

Jacob waved his hands Abot stood in the background holding Jacobs shoulders he appeared to speak in a language yet again total silence Abot spoke to Jacob calling him "Ani is present" Abot told Jacob he was in the corner near the trees telling him not to hold view.

The holograms changed the sun in the background cast different lights Jacob looked the shadows of images changed he looked puzzled he looked at Abot he stood next to Jacob holding his shoulder the animals all bayed the white eyes all glanced in the lowering sun light.

Abot held on to Jacob he was shacking he spoke telling him to speak to the crowd Jacob shouted telling them that Noah had been born with his adorable sister Noi.

A Holo motherhood appeared in the front door she passed in silent words bowed and talked to Noi she touched her forehead whispering words she turned quickly saying "She is perfect" then she spoke of her good spirit. She caressed the floor and walked away Jacob looked from the veranda she vaporized.

Jacob looked confused Abot held his hands saying that it was his daughter that was conceived from the Holo. Abot explained that the person was her Holo mother.

Virtue didn't know of the children the Midwife calmed Jacob and asked him to sit down and speak to her assistant he looked at Jacob and spoke saying that he would not be able to speak of the spirit child. She said a hologram and human hologram had been born it is unknown and Holo cannot be spoken about.

The spirit and Noi had been born delivered while Virtue pass out the child's were placed Jacob saw it and stood cautiously in the door she smiled and laughed Jacob gazed and spoke little the Geminious children had walked away with the spirit Noah he trembled the midwife stood gazed she held his lips everything was held from view a time of truths.

Chapter 17

ABOT SAT AND SMILED SAYING that the celebrations had begun a quiet evening was loomed over the gardens. They could hear the calls the night kept changing the sun had lowered the darkness became Sun light of night almost red glowing softly Virtue became excited and she was sweating she tried to hold the two children laughing with very large pupils they called she sat with rem motion Jacob said holding her hands rather calming ushers.

The crowd had calmed Virtue wanted them to see the children. The ANI sensed the view it darkened Virtue spoke calling her voice wasn't recognized murmurs were heard she announced the name Noi the crowd began to chant music ANI calmly became light the heavens opened cast of coloured Virtue held her head high speaking to Abot he spoke for her.

He asked for the ANI to sleep the crowd in there thousands spoke Jacob stood the lights were brilliances and heavenly music could be heard from Hologram the light became more Jacob spoke a few words then he sat with the child Noah in his lap.

Two children had been thoughtfully introduced to Little York City in England in a park land now owned by Jacob and his new family his spirit friend was also family Jacob bewildered consider what would become of two children one hologram and one human Noah and his spirit would return according to Abot who told Jacob not to ask and wait.

The crowd had looked to see a better view children walked forward to give gifts toys seemed to be in abundance personnel friends collected the two child's laid in there cribs sheepishly crying Jacob spoke to Abot gesturing the night opened the stars shone boats could be heard floating past honking horns and cheering.

The media gathered York TV filmed the whole meeting they were the only team allowed a high priest appeared from the background with a gift he spoke well-being of the child's speaking in English he wished to speak on the veranda Jacob agreed.

The high priest stood and asked everyone to sing a simple song. He started with few words and opened the song of harmony by lowering his voice to get the crowd's voice right. He repeated himself the voices became a single voice as they repeated themselves he raised his arms and waved again with bright eyes and glorious smiles.

The lowering Sun had diminished the night held Transvaal were present eyes seemed to appear humming and animistic sounds were heard the high priest welcomed characters ANI was present he spoke the Universe and sleep of eternity.

Animals appeared in ghost the High priest spoke of the children born stating that the Shpri had transcended and will return to his mother Virtue from distant hologram Suns of Earth.

The night grew festive photos were taken the atmosphere changed through the candle lights and food was served the crowd gathered flowers were given and placed in front of the house. A white dog was on a lead waiting to be gifted. Jacob took on board the dog and thanked the crowd wishing well being for also the gifts he knew its name was Snowball he laughed dear friend!

The heavens opened stars glowed all looked at the colours of the clouds and atmosphere the High priest blessed everyone stating the esrevinv was present it was of course Mother Universe. Light flickered in many different ways silence held moments a few minutes passed then music was played drinks were served the night continued.

Gathering people seemed confused by the night songs were being sung with distant quiet eyes thought well of the park garden animals seemed to be present with interlude sounds.

Jacob walked in his house trying to collaborate a story of his experience he was told that the truth must await otherwise unheard of. He held hands and spoke quickly speaking to Abot he asked for a view of sanity order. Abot sat calm and congratulated

Jacob seeming to change one subject as to define what truth was unheard spoken words.

Speaking in order of unknown languages was unknown to Jacob Abot spoke quietly reassuring him to reason suggesting he took a background view of the occurrence. Jacobs eyes were large he resembled a creature in a darkness of abyss waiting for his next light to surprise.

Pondering for the evening Jacob spoke very few words the gathering had diminished he sat with his very tired wife waiting for his elbows of fall asleep he was alert and concious developing certain tending to lapse in the night.

Chapter 18

THE MORNING ROSE SMALL CHIRPS were heard calling of everyday again Jacob made excuses for a shower peering in the covered light and mirror water cascading he sang a few songs flirting in the mirror with a smile the plan Perfection.

Words of welcoming greets in view a motherly assuming of smiles Jacob asked for breakfast walking in dress he slowly thought to give food his bearings he had seen everything the night before Virtue sat in silence his spoken words were lost in denials.

The news papers had been delivered photos were sprung across the first pages Jacob put them down on the sofa sitting on them Virtue looked guessing he was light-hearted and smiled giving him a nudge offering the child to hold.

The day continued as a silence they were by themselves and related in small ways Virtue was pleased speaking of the children outside the cameras gathered pictures the garden was tidied and Jacob sat next to his mobile phone waiting for difference.

The two twins slept Virtue laid Jacob found himself preoccupied with self relative nothings unsure he sat playing music in his quiet mind Noi and Noah kept the peace the house slumbered in a distant eye with no bearer of spirit he had be taken to the further Sun to be brought back at a later age time prevailed to await.

Jacob knew of the spirit child and assumed he rendered very little to say of him he considered a name to later he waited. 'Sphri' was a perfect name sitting with child's he smiled at Noi she gave him the sense of completion he fell sleep paused his limbs laid the house servant took the children to bed quietly without a sound of animal instinct he awoke snowball wanted attention.

Conversation complied in sleep giving spoken words in sleep itself no one thought to consider a night of fully spoken relents eyes tired less sparkling with white light next to his feet a dog snarled by smiles of lips caressed by air of motherhood waiting for a contemplation a morning of secondary movement birthday balloons bursting to add extra vitality Jacob woke final.

The new days of earlies came to reason life was anew with consider to leaving yourself in an empty corner to suck your thumb and nurture your brain as to reason the universe and two small lifeforms trying to stop the inner bred self of further future calming a driven episode.

Sphri was born in his inspirational way Jacob had seen a child from a motherly apparition with the idea he would return quite when was the question bringing a quite mind was important quiet words would evolve and Sphri would be the first child of the triples Noi was second Virtue passed out during the birth of first calling Jacob to hold moments of the next two.

Virtue rose well the mornings of future dwell in warmth of family occasions brought the two twins together little happened while they ascended to childhood Jacob pleased virtue she smiled and asked questions of the present Jacob gave the future a plan to travel the world.

Teaching the children, Noi had different plans she didn't need a computer she saw everything speaking to Jacob of Sphri and the brilliance of the planet and her soundless sleep quietly speaking of Jacobs story as he continued.

Virtue looked at the relationship as clearly as the marriage took place the high priest merged them after the birth of the children it took ten minutes both were concubine in eternal faith with their very own spirit of all nature the wilderness guided little Noah he spoke wise words always glancing at the windows speaking of human self relating.

Little of age Noah would dance with small steps singing a song called Mr Animal he would harmonise the whole room with silent steps singing with awesome awes standing still to finish with a verse calling the Ani he would then cry and sit in the empty seat given to him a camel hooded seat complaining about the smell of sweat and oil as always he fell asleep with reminding of time and the sun windows as he explored.

Time always passes with congratulating pause the children became as always perfect little darlings confused by the brilliance of the universe offering their little presents a prize in the aftermath of lessons taught by parents to which later became house servants with permanent positions to have all but little to offer except human advice.

The age of children matters is a continuous way creating a path years of year passed Virtue became very fond of Noah they spoke Jacob couldn't wait to write about Noi her knowledge she kept telling him that there was no need to write it she sat in front of the computer with a scrap paper wrote and showed Jacob the library of Noah she laughed and ran to her room it was Noi.

An agreement was always considered a question never availed Jacob sat with rem almost glancing with eyes of fortunes animals roamed his inner mind the spirit he met had become a Holo and Jacob needed to see speak with dimension as to sit in slight tear he wreaked his mind state convinced that he knew Noi touched saying you weep little always he spoke of fluids.

Little England was a place where history takes place of the English pride and justifies all that didn't know otherwise a family gathering to see and UN-see all that created a child of great potential with age he grew to be a student of no other mind but a animal instinct turning away his spirit.

Virtue spoke for the last of years gleaming with smiles of fascination she had created the obvious oblivion she hadn't though so. Jacob wanted to tell her that her children were completing the teen of teen she was unspoken to and Jacob always thought how to tell her that he spirit had vanished and was destined to let her see the truth.

Friends united travel had coursed the land of fame in the few moments they addressed the public in a utmost private way all seemed to be controlled in a sincere ways.

Animals bound their mind to speak of the few ascertained by justice view calmed by Noah they asked quests. The futures appeared later than graces of sun light in morning rises. Noi stood in elements her mind viewed reading of slight religion and yet without.

Noah began claiming his future speaking of authorities he spoke to create a kingdom of lands he bought fields and became obsessed with obtaining land for agriculture and keeping animals with rock houses and hotels schools and holiday resorts to look after animals in all orders. Animal holiday Sanction.

Everyone agreed with the plans nobody spoke otherwise Noah worked too hard Noi laughed in the background Noah's first animals sanction had been developed the rest of the world came to a small conclusion. Sitting every night holding his mothers view he self confided. Jacob grew wary his friend was trying to ask few question.

Chapter 19

ONCE THE FAMILY WENT TO a forest they walked and freely entertained each other Noah walked by him self lost in little confusion walking in to darkness he noticed a stub of tree he sat on it quietly absorbing the sun rays then animals started gathering he chuckled and reassured himself a darkness appeared speaking him name.

The Ani appeared in darkness ushering whispering Shad-dow spoke first. Noah to look under the tree seat he sat Noah couldn't move asking who he was the voice was male and female he smiled at stood the sat as told.

The voice said "This is your book it is called A.B." Noah was told to grow and prune the book in memory of all animals it was Twine Root and the words would appear as it grew. The fruit was water berries Noah store looking he thought he could see eyes he cried and ran in to the nearest light shining.

Noah ran as fast as he could calling Virtue's name he fell twice then he held a branch and smiled shacking his head he looked at the twine book gently he held the letters pruned A.B. Frowning he walked he could smell a distant air instinct was now his elm of future he wiped his eyes and shrugged walking slowly.

He walked through the birds flutters he could smell Virtue he peered through the sun light holding as steady breath listening to his sixth and eighth instinct sense.

Noah found his bound sitting on a rock hill waiting quiet aimless talking to himself many clouds passed a car had spotted him from a car park He laughed at his Mum and Dad and held the book Noi took hold and waved the book in the air.

They drove back home Noi was fascinated she claimed the book had special powers she exclaimed she couldn't read the book she struggled opening it Noah sniggered asking for it back with a side view his eyes glimmered it was a gift he will keep. He described it as a book of letters Noi disagreed.

Noah spoke of a special gift he had been given it was the 'Whispering spirit aura' the ghosts said she would be with him always. She had spoken of his truthful friend who lived in the other Sun of Earth and would return till the time foretold. Scratching his head Jacob drove the children back to York City.

Yorkshire the moment of lowering Sun certain ways of sitting without runners of tiredness wanting the children sat refusing to do anything but wait till the morning.

School was special everyday and yet tomorrow gave music and a sporty mind of relaxing mind taught by a oriental teacher self defence and how to stand still for time of time. Downstairs gave a small room of totality Little movement and plenty of words by the fullest.

Chapter 20

Sphri was becoming of age fifteen to be precise he spoke well of himself and knew time had become to return from the world's of Holo to speak to his parents he had seen them for countless years in observe guiding his Universe to speak of his family.

Three twins would meet, Sphri prepared a meeting in the park speaking of his royal presence sending pictures of himself in mind of Noah the family knew Jacob spoke to Virtue almost in tears and then brushing aside his voice waving gesture till the tomorrows.

Virtue did not sleep she prepared for everything and did not know Jacob was told to wait until the listeners could confirm the child spirit as he was and born with no knowledge of Virtue the night held silence the front gates were opened Virtue asked all lips deceived her very self.

Virtue poor of mind being a totality of mindless wrenched by unknown friend Abbot had spoken her words fell silenced she said she had a cold heart and waited for the food to be prepared she sat on the veranda smoking a cigar it was time the silent one's spoke birds could be heard and seen the park full of virtual reality a slight spirit laid in her unknown eyes.

Jacob spoke Noi stood Jacob looked and smiled she danced otherwise to join her brother she knew very well without she smiled and gestured Jacob, thanked her.

Jacob Our friend we speak of is a presence in your mind he is unspoken and existences in Universal dimension he is your son born first with your sleep you laid he was taken back to diminutive dimension he is a twin he is who the highness.

He wrote to you with picture's of future he is not an elder he is sixteen years old and controls the Hologram Universe in Earth's two Suns guided by personnel of Universe to which he controls. He is always identical and appears to himself with totality and reconcile to his death. His own universe is in his being as a presence to all became.

He also has a twin in Gemini he is identical and they will meet then when time permits. He is very important Noah requires him when destiny claims his life in void of all seen and unseen.

"I've been allowed to tell you by the seers all these years I've known and awaited for apparency I've known of the birth I met the Noah spirit when I met you he was preparing for the ANI the Universe takes all command".

"Sorry" I wait here when is he arriving? In one hour you might see what you cant understand he will be guarded by Holo persons you have never seen or understood their language is telepathic you might hear the Atmos he is very much involved. They will stand in presence.

The family gathered waiting for cars to appear Sphri walked through the main gates looking at the distance he was by himself it seemed Virtue held Jacobs hand she shivered Noi stood in one position slightly smiling Noah approached Virtue stopped him they were told to stand in a certain place the observers needed a clear view.

Virtue laughed and held Sphri hands asking he held his finger to her lips 'You have touched me no others can' Then she saw blue hoods and a black hood in the background she stood back letting go. He smiled and said "They are my Hologram presence he is a 'Ani void' he sees far more so"

'I am your Son born in all dimensions, you slept mother of all mothers you didn't know until now.' I am a spirit now thank you for my short name the sphere knows well that I transported to the eyes of Earth I am not of myself I have many of myself and the Universe is my master " My nick name is 'Joe 90' he laughed heads bowed as earthly smile.

He looked at Noah holding his hand "You have your book" Noi will provide the rest, all in fact! We are brothers your sister is half hologram her perception is beyond the sixth diminutive she is your guide you have a spirit whisper you need to be aware the animals are waiting for you deed do speak to the mind be careful do not claim a mind of Holo we need a animistic viewer and it is you the eclipses will give you aliment.

You are my brother spirit I claimed the destine of few words the begotten are beside me ill await for your reason I call myself 'Small Book'.

The Animals all know of you the light of Sun had called your return to human existence be careful don't be animistic your age of human will await for yourself at age.

In the background the heavens opened spirit stood still speaking of his mind the time has become it is all is spoken the Universe has called it my time here I will be watching you all from the eyes of eyes the elements are returning I must leave to calm the planets a place is always.

Sphri kissed Virtue he held her hands with firm holds ushering I will "be quiet don't doctor Noah" keep him in the garden of book the animals are waiting. Farewell 'Esrevinu' beloved mother Universe.

Virtue watched her son walking away the hoods all stood two blue ones followed he walked through the park dispersing no clouds were present Virtue could hear a rumbling voice then blissfully she cried holding her cheeks turning she passed cameras nothing was recorded spoken was unspoken.

Chapter 21

T HE NIGHT FELL THE NEXT day was an empty view of sun risen by overwhelming concious, Noah had decided that study was not his propriety and his bleak request was to ask others to write with a program called Animal Bible for all artist to diverge attention meanwhile he sat and smoked cigars with a hunger for Greek wine and a little food.

Jacob grew wary of his sons behaviour tending in conversation was little of word the God had started he was only the age of becoming sincere Noah impolite tending to expect all he asked if Noah would tend to the vine twines Noah said Noi was responsible.

Jacob left the house and walked the gardens he asked others the pruning had begun he didn't know who helped. The fact is no one did it grew and grew the twines spread in the few hours Jacob became quite obscure with the story.

Others asked to lay in the garden and sleep. Animals roamed the field was blessed by dying animals three were found one morning Jacob asked for them to be buried the Twine followed writing letters.

The roots of twine wrapped themselves round the animals bringing some of them to the surface little trees began to develop then animals started appearing Jacob insisted Noah worked he walked to the site and spoke firm words enough of all and the pruning began Noah spoke.

Becoming confident hands of others gathered to observe Noah had reserved himself the media wanted to talk he then spoke to Virtue asking which suit to wear he glanced spending thousands of pounds he walked the park and found a cotton shirt it fit him perfectly beloved dustbin it was Noah's the spirit he left a garment in the leather bag loose trousers also thanks to him all those years.

Shaboo Noah wrote a short verse bearing all essentials he smiled a booklet written by human wording to comply with the shabbs of all persons equal to other. Sanity was his aged unknowing he laughed at the brilliant a human Animal character masked by his play.

The due amount from a play scribed by his willing hands Noah tried to reason with a obsession unknown to him he decided to return to his fatherly nature by considering a wife the few he knew gave him pleasure yet of age he sat without knowledge of the child he was sitting waits of torment caused his lonely desolate.

In all time a single Universe become the view for all other Universes and the perfect solution is in light memory and all images focus to create an absolute finding resolution is considered as perfect by all element it means it is what became again in a spiritual way forth.

How then shall the Holo become the nothings of animals seemed to tend to in one way of inner yet the outer experience gave all to the moment of death the gifts of ideal future accorded in slight of eyes.

Sleep of little roamed his mind of leaving Noi told Noah to become a spirit for the subjects of child tending to forgive the gift of life. He tended the twine garden the field was covered with dead animals he worked hard Noi always sat in the distance waiting for the clouds to cast then she would retreat in the basement to draw pictures she invented Hologram she wrote notes with the envious suns.

Computers are technology invented in small pre-portion the Holo isn't acquainted with electric the notion of inventing in Noi view was herself she spoke to soon her mind worked with messages her brother told her little is little Earth bounds her by self view being careful is a priority the void is always empty and quiet no kingdoms.

Noah contemplated the Hologram Religion speak of mind to which Noi was relentless of he thought as to Jacob and questioned Jacob said he thought it was his idea and showed him his book again Noah improved his mind to create the world of in web site form delegating mass of others to write his very own books.

A library was a question of Noi speakingly she shrugged the love of vanishment became self adoration drinking hot chocolate and peanuts night beheld by moment of never entering a room barricaded by evidence her friend in hight spirit driven mad by her half of self to be human Noah gave sight to single and foremost option.

Parents gave all to sitting in lower places of lowering suns drinking huddling excusing the life they never had peoples eyes glanced they hid the garden of Noah had become a graveyard Noi had learnt how to maintain the betweens of caress and poor Jacob had a huge bank account a spirit and a Gemini birthday sat they kissed spirits .

Money became a lesser value endless requests Noah bought lands after lands speaking of building rock hotels and business continued he never went anywhere Virtue drove most of the time she asked what he was happiest doing he said "lovemaking" it was who and he had moved to a house he built Virtue asked for marriage to consider a value in his life.

Besides family the rest of Universe had concluded that the world of Noah had presided in oblivion with endless calls and accusations of blasphemy Noah was on TV and made attempts to write a script for a film Noi wrote the ending and finished it she said the computer spoke to her.

Blue heavens came to mind the attention of sunlight had riddance of wintry inspirit age had become of fortune Virtue had had many ideas and performed artist views in large proportions the world media couldn't doubt her tender welcomes she grew tired Jacob told her to seat and receive her age of reasoning.

A grand master of spirit a universe fulled by a little light a sudden first light the Sphri was present thought of others the time was dear he wanted to explain he aught to present himself an old spirit called Noah he became a presence of universe he sat with unseen Holo's quite perturbed moments away from his mother he couldn't leave aliment the universe need him he would die if so resowed.

Sphri gave reason to Noah he sent holograms to look and record the garden where Noah would rest he prompted the ground to lay his body that wasn't a problem Sphri paced the floor waiting for visuals of England and Noah attempt to create salvations across the world animals thought well walking the grounds and parks organizing everything.

Age became Noah activity he complained about all but the obvious he was married and had adopted two children he lost his virginity at a certain age convenience wasn't a option but his doctor manage to conceive a girl her very angelic self now six and a icon of all the heavens new her well being name Angela.

Noi had thought sitting comfortably with her inspirited friend a boy neighbour speaking of giving the world her money in fact all the money she knew was everyone's she had meetings with people to project there futures she asked the Holo master in silence and the computer sent to all the entities of Earth their projects and the money she smiled.

Chapter 22

Politics Weald the horizons Jacob was concerned the governing bodies didn't know how the Noah family had achieved the accomplishment offered the computers were questioned Noi stood before rooms with congress she encountered for her sheer brilliance and all accounts were neatly placed in order. A man in the corner read her mind he stood with be wishful small speech the court was excused.

No words were spoken of her master plan the authorities asked to observe Noi permitted their assistance the media enjoyed her crusaded in business brilliance she was asked one question always easily answered saying her family 'once existed in a minds view'. She sat often with her house in a sunny place with her child she spoke of all she was human Noi taught nothings allowing her daughter freedom to touch the spirits.

Sheerity of exclusion became masterly the Sphri sat, he decided a tomb would be the ground Noah sat the book would develop round the world twine of water berries would be delivered by beak of birds the peaceful beholding would give light to a memory all animals awaited finding place he would observe his followers absolved the truth of passing years memorising.

A museum lied in the grounds the animals had dug all the rocks held place they made mounds from soil flowers and small trees grew a perfect waterhole with limestone trims underneath the ground crystal clear water Noah didn't know awaiting his reassignments.

Chapter 23

THE CALLS OF PRESENCE WERE awaiting Jacob was old now he had been nursed he wished his final sleep sitting in his seat he could hardly talk and smoked cigars and drank Greek coffee speaking to himself of course he had dementia Sphri tried to help but he had fallen asleep Jacob asked to be left alone his key worker was a young nurse she held his head.

Jacob woke in his death Sphri spoke to him while he slept he passed away he was buried next to his mother a few days later Noi didn't speak for a few years she succeed with Holo and researches progressed she eventually lost her hologram program and retired she was pleased she was human she never travelled she abided with her family happily.

Noah sat in his grave yard he slowly walked he was old and tried to contemplate his mother he slept in Virtues house for years he built a wooden house and complained his family tried to help he was logical yet he travelled time and he fell his balance was uncontrollable his Tomb was ready the religion had bettered his unknowing self.

He was doctored he fell one night Virtue sat cried and she told her short story she only asked Sphri he held her last frail.

Sphri appeared for the last time Noah was in the voids the animal kingdom bowed mercifully spoken with the Hologram Universe all tended as they were always it was exactly the same we are always present nothing ever besides laughter could be heard the Holo always exists.

Noah watched the Animals they walked through the eternal Mister Animal Chuckled muttering Mister Noah's Library.